powerful man in the universe and the protector of Castle Grayskull. Prince Adam's pet tiger Cringer turned into the mighty Battle Cat, He-Man's faithful companion.

Only Orko, the court magician, and Man-at-Arms, He-Man's best friend, knew this secret. Even Prince Adam's parents and Teela, captain of the guard, saw him only as the prince of Eternia. Prince Adam kept his secret because danger lived on Eternia.

On one side of the planet, the sun never shined. There, inside Snake Mountain, the wicked Skeletor planned new ways to find

out Castle Grayskull's secrets. And still others with bad intentions waited on other worlds, ready to disturb Eternia's peaceful way of life.

Against them all stood only He-Man and the Masters of the Universe!

I HAVE THE POWER

Written by Bryce Knorr

Illustrated by Harry J. Quinn and James Holloway

Creative Direction by Jacquelyn A. Lloyd

Design Direction by Ralph E. Eckerstrom

A GOLDEN BOOK

Western Publishing Company, Inc.
Racine, Wisconsin 53404

Library of Congress Catalog Card Number 84-62343
ISBN 0-932631-00-2
A B C D E F G H I J

Classic™ Binding U.S. Patent #4,408,780
Patented in Canada 1984.
Patents in other countries issued or pending.
R. R. Donnelley and Sons Company

Trapped inside the shadows of Snake Mountain, Skeletor's ghostly laugh echoed.

"Behind this curtain stands my greatest invention of evil. Not even He-Man can stop it. At last, I can possess the secrets of Castle Grayskull. I will rule all Eternia!"

"For once in your pitiful life you did as I commanded, Beast Man," Skeletor said.

"But I'm surprised this giant spider didn't capture you. Its brain is obviously much larger than yours."

Skeletor laughed each time the spider fought the force field that trapped it.

"Be gone, Beast Man. I will enjoy my greatest victory alone. Gather my army for the test of my new weapon."

A boney hand opened the curtains. Skeletor turned on a strange red ray. The spider's shell stiffened into the strongest steel. Its legs hardened into metal beams.

"My mechano-ray changes any creature into a living machine," Skeletor said.

"This overgrown bug is now my slave, the unbeatable Spydor. I am so wicked, sometimes I even scare myself."

Inside the palace, the royal circus thrilled King Randor's court. The excited crowd hushed for Eternia's greatest acrobat, "The Human Tornado."

Outside, Skeletor appeared with his army.

"No one will forget your act, Spydor," Skeletor said.

"Let Spydor's test begin!"

Explosions ripped the palace walls! Teela and Man-at-Arms charged outside. Everyone followed, except Prince Adam. He dragged Cringer into a hallway.

"**Come on, Cringer,**" he said.
"**The show has just begun.**"
He drew his Power Sword.
"**By the power of Grayskull,**"
Prince Adam cried.

"I HAVE THE POWER!"

"You are late, He-Man," Skeletor said from atop Spydor.
"We started without you."

Skeletor laughed and fired. He aimed not in He-Man's direction, but toward Teela and Man-at-Arms.

"Take this!" Skeletor's voice boomed.

He-Man leaped and pushed his friends to safety. Spydor's burning rays bounced off the Power Sword and shook the ground. All

around He-Man the fortress crumbled, and the ground below began to open.

He-Man clung to the sides of a growing hole. Skeletor fired again, tearing the Power Sword from He-Man's hand. Battle Cat sprang to help his master and the pit swallowed them both.

"The Power Sword is mine!" Skeletor screamed. He touched the magical weapon, but yelled in pain.

"I must teleport it to Snake Mountain. There I can solve its secrets."

He trapped "The Human Tornado" in Spydor's claws.

"You are my next test," Skeletor said to the frightened acrobat. *"You will lead my final attack!"*

He-Man and Battle Cat fell
far into the palace dungeon.
Their last ounce of strength
stopped the crushing rocks.

With no Power Sword to renew
He-Man's power, they fell fast
asleep. Prince Adam awoke with his
pet snoring at his side.
**"Wake up, Cringer. We must get
out of here,"** he said.

"B-B-But how can we, without your Power Sword?" the frightened tiger asked.

"I don't know, Cringer. We certainly could use the power of the sword."

A wise voice soothed Prince Adam's mind.

"You HAVE the power," the voice said.

Prince Adam felt a friend was near. Could it be?

"Yes, Prince Adam. It is Sorceress."

"Remember the night you and Man-At-Arms first found Castle Grayskull? Remember what I said. Only YOU have the power!"

"I remember it well," Prince Adam said.

"You told me the story of Eternia."

"Once, a long time ago, a wise council ruled the land. All was right. Evil lurked on the planet's night side, held back by the mystic wall.

"But Eternia's rich life spoiled the people.

"You, Sorceress, told the council that the people needed to live on their own again.

   "The council knew evil might break the mystic wall. So all of the council's power became a frightful-looking fortress named Castle Grayskull.

   "One day a champion would claim the power to battle evil."

   "You are that champion!" Sorceress reminded Prince Adam. "Only you have the might to hold the Power Sword."

"Man-at-Arms tried holding the Power Sword first," Prince Adam remembered.

"It burned his hand. But I became He-Man when I held the Power Sword and said 'By the power of Grayskull.'"

"I must go," Sorceress said. "All my strength must stop Skeletor from controlling the Power Sword."

"I DO have the power," Prince Adam said.
**"We can find a way out of here, Cringer.
When we were young, we played
in these tunnels all the time."**

"I'm glad you're not a scaredy
cat," Cringer said. "That would
really scare me."

"He-Man's Power Sword is feeding Spydor," Skeletor laughed.

"When its power is drained, I can control it and learn the secrets of Castle Grayskull. Then we can see what type of machine you make, Human Tornado."

While most of Skeletor's troops celebrated, only two creatures guarded Snake Mountain. Skeletor's laughter made them even more unhappy than they had been.

"Old Skeletor sure is happy," Beast Man said. "Guard duty is my reward for giving him the giant spider."

"Sound the alarm," Mer-Man said. "It's an attack!"

"Calm down," Beast Man said. "That's just a minstrel. Now we can have some fun."

"P-P-Prince A-A-Adam," Cringer whispered. "T-T-This won't work. I don't look like a dancing bear. And your singing is worse than my dancing."

"Greetings, future rulers of Eternia," Prince Adam said. He nudged his pet to keep quiet.

"Celebrate with me and my dancing bear."

While Prince Adam played, Cringer quietly wound his leash around the guards' feet. Prince Adam tugged and Mer-Man and Beast Man fell to the ground.

"Now for my solo," Prince Adam said.

He put an arrow into the guitar and fired. The rope holding the gate to Snake Mountain snapped. The gate slid to the ground, neatly trapping Mer-Man and Beast Man.

Skeletor's laughs led the heroes to the laboratory.

"Skeletor is draining energy from Sorceress and Castle Grayskull," Prince Adam whispered.

"I must get my Power Sword. Soon Spydor will be too strong."

"Sorceress," his mind called. **"Take the sword's power back to Castle Grayskull. Let it go when I tell you."**

"Hurry," Sorceress' tired voice said. "The Power Sword is too mighty to control for long."

The Power Sword's glow dimmed.

"My victory is near!" Skeletor cried.

He grabbed the Power Sword and held it high.

"The Power Sword is mine!"

"Sorceress, let the power return," Prince Adam thought. **"And thanks."**

The full force of Castle Grayskull exploded into the Power Sword. The weapon skidded to Prince Adam as if it had a mind of its own. Skeletor's laboratory was in chaos. Prince Adam used the confusion to grab his Power Sword.

"By the power of Grayskull," he said.

"I HAVE THE POWER!"

A startled Skeletor saw He-Man burst into his laboratory. Skeletor ran to the mechano-ray that trapped the trembling Human Tornado.

"Your skinny sword can't match this!" Skeletor screamed.

The ray shook the acrobat's body as he changed into a living machine. He rose from the ground as Sy-Klone, still human, but with the power of the whirling wind.

"Attack!" ordered Skeletor.

But Sy-Klone did not attack. Instead, he used his whirling action to fly to He-Man.

"Thanks for the new powers, Skeletor," Sy-Klone said. "I've always wanted to fly."

"Your machine doesn't work on humans like it did on that giant spider," He-Man said.

"You can't control Sy-Klone's tornado powers, Skeletor."

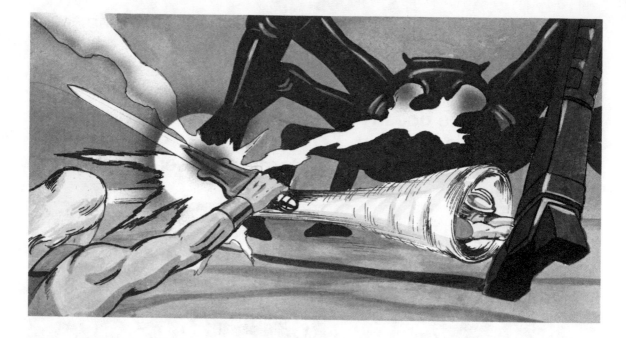

"Then I'll defeat you with Spydor alone," Skeletor said. **"Attack!"**

He-Man blocked Spydor's rays with his Power Sword. Sy-Klone flew around the room to dodge the blasts. Spydor fired wildly, ruining Skeletor's workshop.

"Better put your pet on a leash, Skeletor," He-Man said. **"If you can't do it, we'll give you a hand."**

Sy-Klone grabbed the cord from the curtains. When Spydor's legs were tightly tied, Battle Cat and He-Man tipped it over. Spydor was helpless, but kept firing.

"It's curtains for you, Skeletor," Sy-Klone said.

"We'd like to help you clean up," He-Man laughed.

"But we've got to get Sy-Klone back for his next performance. Lead the way, Battle Cat."

The three raced to the front gate.

"Don't get up," He-Man said to Beast Man and Mer-Man. **"We will let ourselves out."**

Battle Cat broke down the gate with a mighty leap.

"I hope Skeletor doesn't see you two lying down on the job," Sy-Klone said.

Beast Man and Mer-Man struggled to get free. Skeletor's cries came closer and closer.

"That sounds like Skeletor," Mer-Man said. "Now we can get out of here."

But Skeletor was not worried about his guards.

"You fools, you let them get away," Skeletor shouted. **"And He-Man broke my Spydor. It's out of control."**
The mechanical spider crashed towards them. Skeletor freed Beast Man and Mer-Man from their steel jail. When both tried to run away, Skeletor shook his Havoc Staff.

"Come back here and help me capture Spydor," Skeletor ordered.

"I will fix it and rule Eternia."

Beast Man and Mer-Man grumbled, but obeyed.

"What I wouldn't give for a nice giant spider right now," Beast Man sneered.

Skeletor's army slept, tired out from their celebrating. He-Man, Battle Cat and Sy-Klone burst past the army and soon the palace was in sight.

High above, a falcon circled proudly.

"Well done, He-Man," Sorceress said. "And, well done, Prince Adam. You found a way to help Eternia, without the Power Sword."

"Thank you, Sorceress," He-Man said.

"You helped me remember that only I can hold the full strength of the Power Sword.

"I'll never forget that Prince Adam has the power within him, too. We all have power, even if it isn't as much as the power He-Man has."

When the heroes got home, their rest was short. King Randor had a job for his son.

"I forgot about those tunnels, Prince Adam," the king said. "I'm glad He-Man escaped. But I order the dungeon sealed forever! It's too dangerous."

"Prince Adam, take that pet tiger of yours and get the job done."

Prince Adam and Cringer worked hard to seal the dungeon's entrance with heavy rocks.

"Couldn't He-Man help us?" Cringer asked. "My nose is tired."

"This is the last place I want to be," Prince Adam said. **"But someone might see us and learn our secret identities. Prince Adam moves rocks just like He-Man, just not as fast."**

Cringer suddenly jumped into Prince Adam's arms. The fearsome shadow of a giant spider danced on the wall!

"Don't worry, Cringer," Prince Adam said.

He put down his pet and picked up the lantern. Crawling on the glass was a tiny spider.

"You see Cringer," Prince Adam said.

"Not every beast must be defeated by He-Man."

THE END